Terror at the Temple

-Book 3-

Craig Halloran

Terror at the Temple
The Chronicles of Dragon: Book 3
By Craig Halloran
Copyright © March 2013 by Craig Halloran
Print Edition

TWO-TEN BOOK PRESS
P.O. Box 4215, Charleston, WV 25364

ISBN Paperback: 978-0-9896216-2-5
ISBN Ebook: 978-0-9896216-1-8

http://www.thedarkslayer.net

Cover Illustration by David Schmelling
Map by Gillis Bjork
Edited by Cherise Kelley

Publisher's Note
This book is a work of fiction. Names, characters, places, and incidents either are the product of the author's imagination or are used fictitiously, and any resemblance to actual persons, living or dead, events, or locales is entirely coincidental.